A GLORIOUS

Angel Show

Presented

to

_____

Date

_____

A Glorious Angel Show

Copyright © Dandi Daley Mackall
Copyright © Illustrations by Susan Mitchell

Published by Integrity Publishers,
a division of Integrity Media, Inc.,
660 Bakers Bridge Ave., Suite 200, Franklin, TN 37067

HELPING PEOPLE WORLDWIDE EXPERIENCE *the* MANIFEST PRESENCE *of* GOD.

Unless otherwise noted, Scripture quotations are taken from
The New American Standard Bible (NASB), ©1960, 1977 by the Lockman Foundation.
Used by permission.

Library of Congress Cataloging-in-Publication Data [to come]
ISBN 13: 978-1-59145-436-0
ISBN 10: 1-59145-436-6

Printed in China

06 07 08 09 HH 9 8 7 6 5 4 3 2 1

A GLORIOUS

Angel Show

By Dandi Daley Mackall

Illustrated by Susan Mitchell

INTEGRITY®
PUBLISHERS

family

Nashville

The angel came to Mary's house a long, long time ago.

"Mary, you will have a child. I'm here to tell you so!

Name him Jesus. Hold him tight.

He will turn the whole world right."

The angel came to Mary's house a long, long time ago.

The angel came to Joseph's house a long, long time ago.

"Take young Mary as your bride. There's much you need to know.

Love her, keep her by your side.

Raise this child with love and pride."

The angel came to Joseph's house a long, long time ago.

They rode, rode, rode to Bethlehem a long, long way to go.

Caesar said to travel there to pay the tax you owe.

Donkey trotted *clip, clip, clop*.

Miles to go before you stop.

They rode, rode, rode to Bethlehem a long, long way to go.

9

The city filled with crowds and crowds a long, long time ago.

"No more rooms in Bethlehem!" The innkeep told them so.

Mary cried, "This child won't wait!"

Joseph was in such a state.

The city filled with crowds and crowds a long, long time ago.

Shepherds sitting on a hill, a long, long time ago—

Dozing, in the dark, dark night beside the fire glow.

Sleepy shepherds unaware.

Suddenly, the trumpets blare!

In the sky, turned white as snow…

Christ is Lord of everything!

Go and see the newborn king!

Shepherds racing down the hill a long, long time ago.

Wise men journeyed from the East a long, long time ago,

Looking for the King of Kings, searching high and low.

Shining star will light the way,

Angels guiding night and day.

Wise men journeyed from the East a long, long time ago.

Who's that in the stable there, a long, long time ago?

Cows and donkeys *moo-ing*, *braying*, give a big "*Hello*!"

"We made room for you today!"

"In a manger in the hay!"

Jesus in the stable, born a long, long time ago.

The angels came to Bethlehem a long, long time ago.

"We did what we came to do, and now it's time to go."

We'll be watching. Never fear.

Guardian angels, always near.

The angels came to Bethlehem a long, long time ago.

Christ was born in Bethlehem a long, long time ago!

God has sent a Savior, and he wants the world to know.

Jesus Christ is born today!

Come and worship! Come and pray!

Christ was born in Bethlehem a long, long time ago!